World on Fire

WORLD ON FIRE

First edition. September 4, 2023.

ISBN: 979-8223724773

Written by Stephanie Daich.

For Nathan Daich. Thank you for all of your support.

Life

STEPHANIE DAICH
Lost in The Heart of the City

Amongst the crowd at the station
I wander unseen by others.
I smile at blank faces as they pass me,
Yet, no one returns the gesture.
The wind from the tunnel blows my hair
And the smell of urine assaults my senses.
This is my journey as I move about the city.
-Invisible like a shadow.
Loneliness grips me in the sea of humanity.
Do others feel the same way?
I came here with the optimism of changing the world,
Yet, I am the only one who has changed.

Always Chasing Something More

Always chasing, chasing, chasing.
Always chasing something more.
Why do I believe happiness,
Is just beyond the door?
My life is filled with goodness.
I have nothing I deplore.
Yet, instead of enjoying the moment,
I am frowning at the floor.
Why am I keeping track of others,
Trying to even up the score?
I have relatively good health,
Nothing on me is sore.
Why is finding contentment
Such a heavy chore?
Always chasing, chasing, chasing.
Always chasing something more.

The Wasteful Chase of Youth

Another body alteration.
Applying a chemical peel.
The aging process brings frustration.
Never satisfied takes a morbid skill.
Trying to satisfy the youth-obsessed nation.
Snipping or injecting a Botox refill.
Reconstruction by invasive ablation.
Endure the pain for the great revile.
Yet despite your efforts, you'll lose this war.
Desperately grasping your youth from before.

The Most Dangerous

There are odd things done in the sickened mind
By the men who live in deception;
The brain's chambers have their chilling secrets
That would scare you upon inception.
The jails and judges have seen their type,
The men with no conscience to bear.
But the most dangerous,
Is the man that doesn't care.

Telepathy

Presented; a measure of thought.
Implanted in another's head.
Exquisite power.
Divine command unnoticed.
Sensory channels opened.
Physical manipulation
Spectators left baffled.
From one mind to the other.
Ultimate control.

Discipline

Take it to the next level.
DISCIPLINE
Work on despite the burn.
DISCIPLINE
Up before the sun.
DISCIPLINE
Chisel and shape.
DISCIPLINE
Repetition.
DISCIPLINE
Push even when sick.
DISCIPLINE
Sacrifices.
DISCIPLINE
Don't stop.
DISCIPLINE
Pure pleasure.
DISCIPLINE
Progress.
DISCIPLINE
Study.
DISCIPLINE
Reform.
DISCIPLINE
Fire.
DISCIPLINE
Internal will.
DISCIPLINE

Art

Exquisite, hang the color blend high!
The show has it displayed openly,
And many a critic has traveled to see
The image, heavenly;
Within it stirs the emotions trapped
And bursts the entire soul;
The medium, forming dreams
Shall leave the observer whole!

Magical Friend

The words erupt out of the abuser,
As under the table, the child recedes.
Hiding from the pain,
The child clutches prayer beads.
Drift, carry, transform; it's time for a magical friend.
Drift, carry, escape; let the magic begin.
The words disappear to the sky,
As the fantasy friend brings light.
The child, no longer afraid,
Her space feels colorful and bright.
Drift, carry, transform; it's time for a magical friend.
Drift, carry, escape; let the magic begin.
Whenever the world shows cruelty,
The magical friend appears
And takes the child elsewhere,
While eliminating her fears.
Drift, carry, transform; it's time for a magical friend.
Drift, carry, escape; let the magic begin.

Only a Memory and Nothing More

While through the high school halls, I stroll, awakened, ghosts touch
my soul.
Where were my friends from the past? What happened to those times
before?
As I recall, nearly dreaming, recollections flood in, powerfully
streaming.
In my mind, recalling, enthralling times behind the classroom door-
"Tis only a memory," I mutter, "school was such a chore-
Only a memory and nothing more."

Then my anger flared, thinking, those bullies made me scared.
Here is where my test was given, studying hard for the score.
Thinking of teachers, my muscles tightened, hours of lectures, my
mind enlightened.
In my past, I tried climbing, climbing up the social ranks-
"Tis only a memory," I mutter, "trying to climb the ranks-
Only a memory and nothing more."

When in my eyes swells the tears, reminiscing my teenage years.
These halls knew joy and pain -so many emotions kept in store.
Leaving the school, I'm bawling. Years of memories return calling.
In my car, as I am driving, driving lost in my head-
"Tis only a memory," I mutter, "repeating in my head-
Only a memory and nothing more."

Move. Muscle, Move

The heavy work falls on bended knees
In numbing hours of repetition.
More fun activities lost across time,
As your will held in submission.
Move, muscles, move, as muscle memory forms.
Move, muscles, strengthen; muscles creating new norms.
The pain, the strain, the loss of hours;
Yet, something more grows within.
As mind reshapes, the body learns,
The lazy ways turn to discipline.
Move, muscles, move, as muscle memory forms.
Move, muscles, strengthen; muscles creating new norms.
And at the start, the goal so distant.
Yet every day, you grow a little faster.
The body/mind has etched a skill
Then one day, you are a master!
Move, muscles, move, as muscle memory forms.
Move, muscles, strengthen; muscles creating new norms.

The Comedian

Up from the garbage-filled slums on the street,
Pushing through obstacles of disparity and hardship,
Stumbling over impossible barriers,
Rises, the stand-up comedian,
Ready to break the chains.
Warn out from rejection or, perhaps life,
Yet, with no other escape from the street,
He swallows his pride and hides his fear,
Like an actor pretending he's unscathed,
Trying to break the limitations.
Another club, a dingy bar, all darkening his soul.
Hackers and jerks shouting words of hate,
He bravely dons his mask that hides his defeat,
And he continues with his wit and roasts,
While dying on the inside.
Down to the basement of his childhood home,
Searching through comedy skits and shows,
Tripping his lines, then making them better,
Pouring over books and podcasts,
Dedicated, he masters the craft.

Iceman

Inside the frozen pond
He submerges in the ice
Breathing keeps him warm

Infinity of Thought

As thought moves across the Celestial Sphere,
As sounds vibrate that only you hear,
As new ideas plant their seed,
It's time to listen and take heed.
The infinity of thought is boundless.
The ideas ruminating are often soundless.
Answering its persistent call.
Surrendering yourself to its all.

Death

Death takes who he wants.
Death doesn't care.
Death does not negotiate.
Death is ruthless.
One cannot bargain with Death.
One cannot change Death's mind.
One cannot hide from Death.
One cannot stop Death's path.
Death does not respect persons.
Death could care less about race.
Death has his plans.
Death always wins.

Independence Day

Explosion vibrating through my chest
Colors bursting in the dark celestial sky
Music blasting patriotic songs
Pride surfacing from my core
Freedom celebrating all around me
-Happy Independence Day!

Get a Dog

Get a dog- they begged.
We need it.
Get a dog- they pleaded.
We'll care for it.
Get a dog- they cried.
We'll walk it.
I got the dog
He tore apart my furniture.
I got the dog.
I stepped in a pile of poop.
I got the dog.
I take him for his walks.
They don't play with the dog.
They are at school.
They don't notice the dog.
They are atthe the club.
They don't care for the dog.
They moved out.
It's just me and the dog.
I fell in love.
It's just me and the dog.
He's my companion.
It's just me and the dog.
He's all I have left.

How Can it End so Quickly

The high carries the soul across mountains.
Nothing in life can be greater than now.
Not even nectar can be this sweet.
But the lightning flashes.
The thunder crashes.
And then.
It's gone.

Already Done

We think we are unique.
But it's already been done.
We believe our feelings are single.
We suffer in silence.
We rejoice out loud.
We sin.
We follow unknown paths.
We delight in pleasure.
We shrink from responsibility.
We think we are unique.
But it's already been done.

Passage of Time

My stress! My anxiety! My calm!
O the ticking of the clock,
The passage of the meter.
Who's there to speed up time when everything is wrong?
Who's there to slow the minutes when joy reaches its peak?
O time! O hours! O regime!
To hold you in my hand, the rhythm of the world.
The week will never end, yet the months have flown by.
The deadline snuck behind me, with so much to do.
O month! O year! O eternity!
Now, all is a big blur.
For me, the memory is here—for me, the time is gone.
For the lonely, time does suffer them—ALL seems to have moved on.
Stop the clock! Rush the day. Where did the time go?

Ingratitude

Prosperity abounds in us,
Even found among the poor.
Our generation has much more,
Then our ancestors before.
Our heaters burn night and day,
And the air conditioner is always blowing.
We control our thermostats perfectly,
While our lights are always glowing.
Our cupboards and refrigerators,
Hold our favorite treats.
We didn't have to grow or can
Our supply of fruits and meats.
Technology is at our fingertips,
Information on a whim.
We can be whoever we want,
No longer expected to be proper and trim.
We have so much and are so blessed,
Yet, we can hardly see,
The abundance that today offers us.
And yet, we are as empty as can be.

Creative Side

When I open the creative side,
The neurons firing within,
Burning ideas like flames consuming,
That's when ideas begin.
And when I open myself to the genius,
The humming of the brain in motion,
Breaking out from the stagnant,
My attention turns to devotion.
That's when my dreams come alive,
As my hands and mind create.
Consumed by the processes,
The rest of my life forced to wait.

Fast Rode the Teen

With hope, strong and giving,
Ever waving a strong will
To stand on their own,
Fast rode the teen
And entered the social scene
Ready to find acceptance
To prove their own.
Fast rode the teen
Determined to conquer the world
Fighting, learning, and taking
To hold their own.

Ility

To reach accomplishment/one must be competent
-ABILITY
Regarding others/caring for strangers and brothers
-CIVILITY
Virtually elegant/kind sweet temperament
-GENTILITY
Lacking pride/personal wants to push aside
-HUMILITY
Quality behavior/being someone's exalted savior
-NOBILITY
Free of stress/peace to bless
-TRANQUILITY

Trapped

I feel trapped//. Inside my home.
I want to escape//. I need to roam.
These four walls keep me closed in.
There is no future//. Only the has-been.
The time to leave is now.

Adulting

Remember in childhood.
How free, we didn't realize.
We longed to reach adulthood.
Unaware of its surprise.
Adulthood is drudgery.
To-do lists growing longer.
Free time is a luxury.
Depression growing stronger.
Time to focus mindfulness.
Allowing stress to release.
Adulting is frightfulness.
As life and talents decrease.
Don't live life with idleness.
Each moment is a treasure.
Grab life as a lioness.
Make adulting your new pleasure.

Sound

Vibration: Booming of thunder from the almighty Fighter Jets
Challenge: Deep Exhaling and Heavy Breathing
Always in the background: Zooming of Cars
Peaceful feeling of home: Cooing of Dove
Busy at work: Clicking of a Keyboard
Power: A Body Slamming in the Ring
Tranquility: The Rustling of a Breeze
Pure serendipity: Children Laughing
Angry emotions: Car Horn Blaring
Nerves on end: Children Fighting
Pure comfort: Tweeting of Birds
Strangers Beware: Dog Barking
Alert: Creek of a Home
The sound of love: Kiss

Superposition

Trying to measure Einstein's theory of gravity can fail,
Because it's hard to control each detail.
Since magnetic fields do interrupt,
Therefore the findings are corrupt.
Is there a way to probe gravitational forces?
How about we change the atom's measurement courses?
Superposition is the newest test,
Where there's more control and less stress.
Physicists split the atom apart.
Their differences they do chart.
Superposition better measures the gravitational field.
With more accurate measurements revealed.

Floating Cube

Presented: a floating cube.
The work of great craftsmanship.
Exquisite to behold.
One can easily appraise by a visual over.
But they would undervalue.
The inner of the cube holds infinitely more.
Layers tucked deeply within.
Rich beauty folded in gyri and sulci of personality.
Passion and caring.
Giving and sharing.
Sacrifices and humility.
Pride and strength.
Talents and knowledge.
Hard work and perseverance.
Ambition and goals.
Selfless.
Self-giving.
Genuine.
Heartfelt.
Experience and pain.
Yet, only the inner surface.
Depths of amazement to discover.
Delight continues to increase,
As the workings of the cube come forth.

Solitary Confinement

23 hours alone in a room.
Such a life feels one with gloom.
A small dog run; an hour out.
Only an hour to move about.
The mind plays tricks like hallucinations.
Often switching into derealization.
Such a living would make hell look nice.
Death would feel worth the price.
Stuck in confinement, the soul does dwindle.
What one would give for a window?
Solitary confinement; a torturous state.
Pray that it will never be your fate.

They Preserve it All

When fruit ripens on the tree,
As honey is produced by the bee,
And the ground gives its yield,
A splendid sight in the field.
The preservationist readies their kitchen.
With neighbors and family ready to pitch-in.
Harvest time, close to fall.
Working hard, they preserve it all.

Today

A-Z Today

A culture
　　Building upon vanity, materialism, sex

Children lead astray by confusing messages

Drugs poisoning bodies and minds

Egos puffed up

Families falling apart

Gangs running the streets

Hollywood setting the standard, not the home

Irresponsible parents

Jails overcrowded

Killings on the rise

L OVE; CAN IT BRING IT BACK?

M issionaries spreading good and aid.
　　Nurses and doctors serving others.

Open hands and open donations

Preachers teaching about God

Quotas surpassed as charity is raised

Rescue houses opening their doors

Service done to bless

Teachers passing on knowledge and skills

Unifying organizations giving time

Voices standing up for the abused

Windows of opportunity opening

Xtra supplies sent to the poor

Young adults serving the elderly

Zest and joy for righteous living

Star Trek Commemoration

O Trekkies! O Trekkies! Rise up and celebrate.
For you 55 years of devotion—for you dedicated emotion.
For your call, to a genius mind, Gene Roddenberry, a scientific
magnate.
Here Trekkies! -Star Trek elation!
Nine series filled your head.
A science-fiction foundation,
Millions of imaginations fed.
Star Trek! Held a 55-year duration.
Star Trek Day to coordinate; the "Boldy Go" campaign to
commemorate.
For you 55 years of devotion—for you, dedicated emotion.
O Trekkies! O Trekkies! Rise up and celebrate.

Dungeon and Dragons Call

As the Dungeon Master keeps control,
As the players morph into their roll,
As a new world manifests,
Time to enter the fantasy quests.
The use of strategy is complex.
Using magic or a hex.
Answering Dungeon and Dragon's call.
Surrendering yourself to its all.

Talisman Sabre

China's ships lurk around the corner.
Watching from the bay; stealthy foreigner.
TALISMAN SABRE. TALISMAN SABRE.
The US and Australia working together.
Hand and hand; Freedom forever.
TALISMAN SABRE. TALISMAN SABRE

50 Liters a Day

Cape Town, South Africa, is in a drought.
Every drop of water they must measure out.
People only get fifty liters a day.
Of water, they don't waste much away.
Those who take too much are publicly shamed.
Usage has dropped. They don't want to be blamed.
Neighbors keep close eyes out for water waste.
If one uses too much, they are fined and disgraced.
In America, water runs in the gutter.
While liters and liters, the sprinklers sputter.
The showers tend to flow as long as one wishes.
Consumption isn't confined to 50-liter dishes.
Cape Town is trying to get by on water so little.
The thirsty people are forced to drink their spittle.
They have managed to conserve their small supply.
They have to conserve, or everything will die.

Mental Health

Into the Shadows He Hides

Wiggling and burning in the conscious eye,

The sinner hides from his sin.

Life falls apart. Spun are the lies.

Deception loosed upon others.

Crimson is the blood that drips from the soul.

Tainted the man has become.

Passion has led from his heart.

Indeed, he will soon be discovered.

Yet, he goes on covering his wrongs.

-Trying to live in both worlds.

He wants what he has but covets yours.

And he damages others to hold onto both.

Darkness showed his wicked heart.

Into the shadows, he hides.

While his deceit he wears on his sleeves.

He is pitiful.

He is me.

My Most Intimate Friend

Dear Mental Illness,
There is no one out there that I am closer to.
You have attached yourself to me.
-tightly
You never leave.
Sometimes, you quietly remain in the background,
Making me feel as if I am in charge.
But I am not.
You are.
And have been for years.
Relationships are complicated, and inevitably, they end.
Everyone leaves me.
But not you.
You, you bastard,
You are always there.
You have clung tighter to me than even my parents have.
You make your presence known in large crowds.
I can't shake you.
I should be honored that you are always with me.
But I am not.
You know me better than I know myself.
You must love me to dedicate yourself to me,
To show me such fierce devotion.
I have never had a more intimate relationship with another than with
you.
You know every inch of my body,
For you remind me of my imperfections.
You know all my damning thoughts,
And use them against me.

I have tried to break up with you time and time again,
But you won't let me.
You cling to me.
Your very existence depends on me.
Mental illness, you are my loyalist friend.
I know you will be with me until I die.

How

How do you keep your head above the crowd
-when the noise around is loud?
How do you shine bright
-when life extinguishes your light?
How do you show you care
-when your burdens are hard to bear?
How do you continue on
-when your will is gone?

Astray

I lost myself,
As I chased a dream,
A dream filled with deceptive steam.
I deceived myself,
As I closed my eyes,
Eyes clouded by a web of lies.
I lied to myself,
As I sold my soul,
A soul tarnished as black as coal.
I tarnished myself,
As I gave my will,
A will chained to the forbidden thrill.
I chained myself,
As I lost my way.
A way and soul that has gone astray.

I'm Leaving You for Sure

I love you.
I do. I truly, genuinely love you.
I have tried to hide my love.
I have denied it.
I am dependent on you.
I rely on you to fill an emptiness.
I didn't think I needed you, but I do.
When we are taking distance from each other, I see you everywhere.
EVERYWHERE!!!
In every place.
You are impossible to avoid.
Whenever I take a break from you, I'm left wanting more.
I didn't ever want to admit it.
But I am addicted to you.
You thrill me more than anything else in life.
You make me happy.
You make me feel good.
But there are red flags with you.
Others have pointed them out.
But I ignore all those warnings.
I want to think with me that you are different.
How can what they say be right when you make me feel so good?
Sometimes, I am fully aware of the negative way you treat me.
But I struggle to let you go.
How can I move on without you?
I have tried before. But your hold on me is like chains.
I am addicted to you.
I need you.
I love you.

I want you.
But...you keep hurting me.
If I want what's best for me, I must leave you.
Permanently.
It is so hard to leave you.
I have loved you for so long.
But I must.
So, this time it is for sure.
This time, I will not cave to your beauty,
to your intoxication.
I am leaving you for sure this time.
I am breaking the control you have over me.
It is time for me to say,
Go to hell, Sugar!

Behind a Mask I Hide

-You see me.
I wear a mask.
Designed to deceive.
-You see me.
My life is lies.
I make you believe.
-You see me.
If you knew the real me.
You might grieve.
-You see me.
A heart of stone.
It would make you want to retrieve.
-You see me.
My intentions a web of tangle.
No good I hardly achieve.
-You see me.
But you don't know me.
My goodness, you misconceive.

Within

As the fire burns within,
As I alone know of my sin,
As I pretend that all is well,
My inner self transverses through hell.
Confidence might define my stride.
Yet inside my infernal I hide.
Once discovered, I'll take the fall.
Then I stand to lose it all.

Demon

Is the demon in your head telling truth?
Did you forget he was a lying sleuth?
His words never end; he is always with you.
Did anyone else proclaim words that were true?
Did you find yourself alone in the night?
Or trapped in fear without the light?
What kind of hold does your demonic friend elicit?
Why is your faith in his words implicit?
Can you say that your friends thought about you today?
Why does the demon fill the space when they are away?
Why does the demon never leave?
He is there to help when you grieve.
You say you want the demon to let you be.
But that bastard never does flee.
Then you realize the demon knows you better than all.
The demon is there; you don't have to call.
Why does your demon never abandon your side?
Why can't you banish him? You have tried.
Why has he stayed your whole mortality?
Why will the demon never set you free?

Two Spirits Fought Inside of Me

Two spirits fought inside of me,
To control my single vessel,
And each one fought to be free.
One spirit kind, the other angry.
-inside a mighty wrestle.
When the kind one took the reign,
To others, I treated with care,
And from vices, I did abstain,
As my love took domain,
With the kind spirit, I acted fair.
But the angry spirit did hate,
In my vessel, he made it dark,
And toil and confusion he did create,
leaving me in a compromised state.
With him there, life fell apart.

Confusion

Confusion came long ago,
Speaking to the hearts of man.
It spread disarray across the centuries,
Creating misery and woe.
It told some truths, that seemed to ring true,
Luring Its victims in.
Stroking hate and anger around,
As the dissonance grew.
Beguiled and doped, man did engage,
Of Its devious plan.
Man allowed the monster in,
Filling man's peace with rage.

The Chosen One

He came to me in the mid of the night,
Entering into my room.
For others, it might have brought them a fright.
This creature from another realm.
But I had waited for his call,
Always knowing he would come
To sweep me away from humanity's all,
For I was the chosen one.
His form, unlike my own,
Made of plasma and light.
His strange voice and language to me unknown.
Yet still, I was not scared.
He used a rod and zapped my head.
His lightning shocked my senses.
In my body, the darkness spread.
Until later, I awoke alone.
I think it's been years since that dreadful day,
When my liberty he did steal.
When that creature whisked me away
And locked me in this cage.
Unthinkable experiments he's done to me
as my body and mind, he has tortured.
If only he would let me free,
So I could return to my realm.
I guess it's my fault, for I foolishly believed.
His realm offered me greatness.
This hell I had not conceived.
Me, the chosen one.

Tragic End

The body submits
"I can't resist your power"
and in an instant
twelve years of sobriety
has come to a tragic end

Absorbed by

Sadness, the loss of a day.
Sadness, do go away.

To Hide

Darkness in the night
A loud bump under the bed
come to steal my soul
I must find a place to hide
-To hide from my own wickedness.

Self Improvement

Altruism

Seize the day, when you put someone else first.
Altruism.
The top of Maslow's pyramid.
Altruism.
Seize the day, when you give of yourself for another.
Altruism.
Ignoring your hurt as you balm another's pain.
Altruism.
Seize the day, caring for someone without an alternative motive.
Altruism.
The greatest achievement one can meet.
Altruism.
Seize the day and find someone to serve.
Altruism.

Hope

HOLD ME, HOPE

Hope, entertain me a little while there is still room to grow:
Keep me here, and when it is time, my destiny, you must show.
It could be the place, it could be the time, as you lead me along,
Swirling around me, calling me with your song.
Ambition, around the corner, overlooking the stagnant life.
Ambition, killing the complacent, overtaking the strife.
Many a night in my dreams, you call me,
Promising to set me free.
Many a night you, show me a better way.
Yet, you seem to disappear the very next day.
I am here, dear Hope, open to you.
I am here. Please show me what to do.
Yet, Hope, you are easily dashed against the rock.
While negative influences, your pathway they block.
Hope, you have the power to lift me high.
Yet, you abandon me and leave me dry.
Hope, how you make life bright and kind
Yet, in many corners you are hard to find.
When I cling to you, Hope, you motivate me.
When I trust in you, you set me free.
But more often than not, you are hard to find.
Sometimes, you're gone when I am lost in my mind.
Life is better with you by my side.
When you are here, my fears subside.
I need you, Hope; please stay with me.
Hold me Hope; help me to see.

Always

Always offer kindness,
Always share your soul,
Always open your heart,
And always aim for a goal.
Work on self-improvement,
Work on home and land,
Work to build a better place,
And work to lend a hand.
Often offer kindness,
Often self-reflect,
Often hold the doors for others,
And often give respect.
Strive to lift another,
Strive to be your best,
Strive for an education,
And then you will be blessed.

The Call

The call has planted its seed,
And with great fervor, embedded its plan.
Has been clearing out the cobwebs
And unthawing the frozen man.
Every roadblock must be cleared.
Woe, the obstacles overwhelm
And the weakest link must be fixed
To enter the new realm.
From doubts with powerful opposition,
Chains the man to low expectations.
The stiffening hold of regression,
Locks him in unfavorable stations.
He once had a will and a power.
Energy and joy was his daily song,
But somewhere in life, it diminished
While laziness guides him along.
He can be more than he became.
A warrior turned to sludge.
Out of the hole, he must climb
Releasing the innermost drudge.
Can the call be enough for the man,
The will to try something new?
A cleansing of the soul.
To his whole self, he must be true.
The call has buried its seed,
While hope waters the plan.
It takes discipline and great work,
To rebuild the dying man.
The refurbished man can be great,

Ignoring the desire to quit.
He must resculpt his ambitions
And be willing to commit.
The storms will beat this man,
Throwing hailstorms and rain.
He must ignore them all,
While for greatness, he does train.
The closer he gets to his goal,
The stronger his body will be.
A strength inside has built,
While the quitter inside him will flee.
The call has planted its seed,
And with great fervor, embedded its plan.
Has been clearing out the cobwebs
And unthawing the frozen man.

Hope

I.
The hope buried below the surface
Who
Offers to those with nothing left a
Glimmer
Of something better.
I.
The light in the dark
Who
Offers a way for those
Blinded
By the darkness.

Excitement

Excitement! would I carry you around-
Always in every moment,
Your joy not to be drowned,
Upon me, your bestowment.
The flowing hormones of exhilaration,
Of pure euphoria taking hold,
Of life full of elation,
Within me, you unfold.

Love Yourself

Your value is there.
Believe in yourself.
Have an attitude of self-respect.
Consider your greatness.
Treasure your uniqueness.
Hold confidence in your abilities.
Appreciate your shortcomings- they help you learn.
Declare your worth.
Evaluate your needs for growth.
Walk with confidence.
Rise with importance.
Open to learning.
Feel other's love for you.
Understand who you are.
Grow with change.
Become your best.

Be Your Own

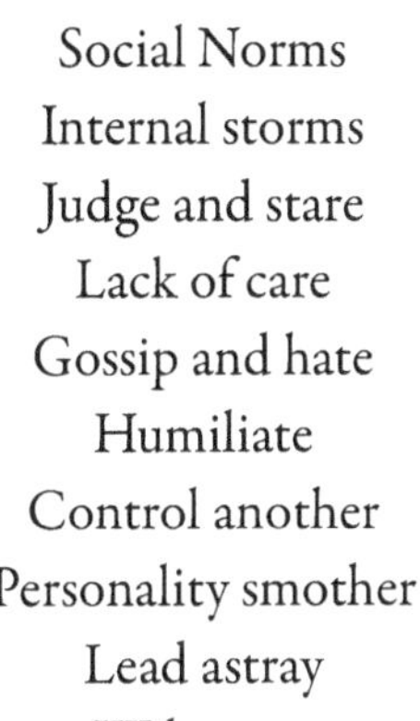

Social Norms
Internal storms
Judge and stare
Lack of care
Gossip and hate
Humiliate
Control another
Personality smother
Lead astray
Wilt away

Must break free
Allowed to be
Self empower
Do not cower
No longer care
When others impair
Be your own
Your will is known
Personality blossom
You are awesome

Goals

My goals I pose to me alone,
yet their reach affects the others.
Then, way too quickly, my goals are blown.
Willpower, myself, often smothers.
Failure, I've already sown.
Defeat, mine or another's.
Why do I listen, why do I hone?
I'd think I'd control my druthers.
I silence the naysayers,
No longer willing to surrender,
I release negative layers,
And become my goal's defender.

Your Accountability

Why do you sit there mad at the world?
Why do you blame others but never yourself?
Do you feel the world owes you something?
Do you not see you owe the world?
Can't you see the good that is around you?
Can't you recognize your abundant opportunities?
How did you get so lost in self-pity?
How did your attitude get this negative?
Is your plight the only one that matters?
Are your needs higher than others?
Should you not lift a finger to help yourself?
Should you not earn your way?
Will you ever put forth the effort?
Will you ever give what you can?
When will you rise on your own?
When will you take accountability?

O Self! My Self. Rise Up and Lend a Hand

My compassion! My conscious! My soul!
O the crying of the wounded,
The desolate left alone.
Who's there to balm their broken heart?
O Self! My self! Rise up and lend a hand.
Show up—for you, the call is here—for you, the time is now;
In the gutter, the forsaken suffers—YOU have much to give;
Take the call! Hear the call! If you don't serve, then who does?
O Self! My self! Rise up and lend a hand.
O Self! My self! Give healing across the land.

Relationships

It's too Much Work to be Your Friend

You say you're my friend, but you don't call.
You say you're my friend, but I am alone when I fall.
You talk, and you share, but you never inquire.
With them, you stay out late, but with me, you retire.
I'd walk away now, but then you give just a little.
It's hardly much, nothing committal.
I give you the bulk of my friendship heart.
But carelessly, you shred it apart.
I like you, but this hurts, so I don't need you.
From the hurt, I decide we are through,
but then you send just a little my way.
It's never much, just enough to bait me to stay.
Why in our friendship must there be games?
The inconsistency feels like daggers and flames.
I am straightforward. You'll get what you see.
But the next time we meet, I never know who you'll be.
Will you smile when I walk into the room?
Or turn away quickly, feeling me with doom.
Sometimes, you welcome me into your personal bubble.
Other times to stand by you seems like so much trouble.
It's too much work to be your friend.
I think it's time to let it end.

Loved by You

It was, it feels, thousands of years ago,
In a home you built with love, I grew,
Where my childhood played in those walls,
Where I was loved by you;
With a fondness of heaven's touch,
You, my parent; kind and true.
It was, in those walls, long ago,
You taught me how to live, I grew,
And you had patience for all I did,
There I was loved by you;
And you sacrificed all you had for me,
You, my parent; kind and true.
It is, in my heart, memories abound,
You gave me support and safety, and I grew,
And you showed me how to care for others.
I know I am always loved by you;
I will hold gratitude for what you gave me.
You, my parent; kind and true.

You Made Me Whole

When we bonded
And molded as one,
My spirit responded
You were the one.
Electric tingled within me,
Warmth from your touch,
Truly we were meant to be.
I loved you so much.
The sun rising in the sky,
The flowers in the field,
The butterflies flying by,
My broken heart healed.
You made everything brighter.
You warmed my soul.
My burdens seemed lighter
You made me whole.

Life of Disgrace

I've done what I did.
From my sins, I have hid.
My staining, I can't rid.
My lies, turbid.
I took, and I stole.
My intentions, dark as coal.
Buried myself in a hole.
I've sold my soul.
I can't reclaim what I've lost.
Carelessly tossed,
The deception does exhaust.
Bad feelings now crossed.
I'd ask for your grace,
For my life of disgrace.
But I must embrace
My personal abase.

Creating New Boundaries

From commitment hour, I am not true.
As others saw-I cannot do
As others-I cannot calm
My disappointments, I cannot balm.
From the same upbringing, I do not hold.
My fulfillment-left untold
My satisfaction-left unchecked
To them, I'm a defect.
Then-in my life, new friends I meet.
My brokenness-they complete
My outcast-they include
My life; renewed.
To some groups, I am stained.
A relationship-strained
A loyalty-never formed
Always theatrics performed.
Yet out there are those who appreciate.
Caring for me-or my fate.
Caring for me-they give me all.
They invite, include, and call.
From this insight, I will no longer give.
My heart and time-to those who don't forgive.
My heart and time-to those who defame,
And tarnish my name.
My time I'll give to those who care.
Loving and kind-I'll follow anywhere.
Loving and kind-to them I'll unite.
Forming a friendship solid and tight.

ABC Family

A fan, a friend, an enemy.
A parent to a child, sometimes considered a frenemy.
A relationship, a bond of clemency.
Banded together by maternal ties.
Broken relationships from mounds of lies.
Building trust with compromise.
Children trust and follow parents anywhere.
Controlling parents are hard to bear.
Coming together in family prayer.
Dancing, imagination, family time.
Discovering hobbies, together they climb.
Drudgery, work, cleaning the grime.
Effort is made to communicate.
Evoking love, causing hate.
Endless battles, judge and berate.
Fluctuated emotions, a bumpy ride.
Forgiving each other, relinquishing pride.
Forging forward or taking a backslide.
Gaining respect and understanding.
Gruff and demanding.
Gentle and kindness expanding.
Harrowed times raising teens.
Heredity passed through the genes.
Hurt and humiliation often unseen.
Ignoring the things that make one mad.
Imparting kindness when another is sad.
Idolizing one's mom or dad.
Joining together, becoming one.
Jilted, ready to be done.

Joyous daughter; wonderful son.
Kindness given even when it is hard.
Keeping the distance, upholding the guard.
Kicking the ball out in the yard.
Living together, getting along.
Learning the words to the family song.
Lessons on how to belong.
Maximizing each paycheck.
Meaningful words, tolerance, and respect.
Messy car; house a wreck.
Nice words shared day and night.
Nagging to the verge of a fight.
Nurturing, making the future bright.
Oasis, away from the storm.
Outstanding, better than the norm.
Omitting the will, learning to transform.
Playing and finding joy.
Pestering, teasing, trying to annoy.
Pride in the baby girl and boy.
Quality time brings the family near.
Quarreling, filling one with fear.
Quiet moments, sweet and dear.
Reasonable expectations.
Rocking away at the foundations.
Respecting for the older generations.
Supporting each other no matter the cost.
Seeking and balming the broken and lost.
Serving to the point of exhaust.
Tolerance toward each other.
Treasured role, father-mother.
Teaching love between sister and brother.
Ultimate sacrifice of ambitions.

Unqualified people thrown into the position.
Understanding your partner's tradition.
Vigilant parents staying the course.
Virtue and rules trying to enforce.
Vanishing values lead to divorce.
Whimsical memories made along the way.
Wanting the children to listen and obey.
Wakeless nights and an extra-long day.
Xenial friendship between parent and child.
Xenacious relationships and disappointment compiled.
XOXOXO –love undefiled.
Young parents growing old fast.
Yielding to your child, putting yourself last.
Yesterday feelings lost in the past.
Zany families as odd as can be.
Zealot parents no longer carefree.
Zest of life found in the family.

Parenthood-

Given trust over another human's life.
Educating.
Teaching.
Sharing talents.
Molding.
Patience.
Sacrifice.
Hurt.
Joy.
Unconditional love.
Holding tight.
Letting go.
Cuddles.
Love.
Kisses.
Power.
Creation.
Dream.
Aspire.
Challenges.
Crying.
Dreaming.
Learning.
Messing up.
Giving.
Taking.
Breaking.
Peace.
Confusion.

Balance.

Insecurities.

Lost.

Found.

Bold.

Timid.

Out of control.

Alone.

Embrace.

Hero.

Villain.

Sleepless.

Hurting.

Soaring.

The greatest hell you'll ever go through.

Untrue as a Heart Of Lies

Out of my thoughts that consume me
Untrue as a heart of lies
I drop to a bended knee
And cover my sinful eyes
In the moments that define me
I've shown my colors true
I've set my passions free
I've allowed my darkness through
Beyond the settled dust
My consequences collected
I left a trail of distrust
My life forever affected

Gossip, Slander, Gossip

The hypocrisy drips off your pious face.
Your mask twisted in a smile.
It's not genuine; you do it all for show.
Yet, behind my back, you're ugly and vile.
Gossip, slander, gossip. Did you forget the golden rule?
Gossip, slander, stab; your ways are so cruel.

You and I, we both sin,
Yet mine you criticize.
Each of us stumbles and falls.
But my name, you hurt with lies.
Gossip, slander, gossip. Did you forget the golden rule?
Gossip, slander, stab; your ways are so cruel.

Although you've wrecked my name,
To anyone who'll listen.
I'll choose the better way.
I'll be the only Christian.
Gossip, slander, gossip. Did you forget the golden rule?
Gossip, slander, stab; your ways are so cruel.

When the Love is Gone

How do you stay when the love's gone?
How do you endure another love song?
How do you care when you're alone?
-When your deepest desires are never known.
How do you smile when unsupported?
The joy is dim, no longer courted.
How do you pretend that all is well,
When staying together only feels like hell?
How do you act like all is grand?
-When no one is there to hold your hand.
How do you stay when the love's gone?
It's time for you to move on.

I Know it Hurts My Child

I will protect you, my child.
I will protect you, my child.
I am here.
I know your mommy is gone.
I can't say why.
But, know you did nothing wrong.
We are not as strong on our own.
I didn't count on this.
I didn't see it coming.
I promised you a family at your birth.
And now it was taken from us.
We are still a family, just broken.
But we will heal.
I know it hurts.
I know it's hard.
I see the pain on your face.
It's okay to feel.
I feel as well.
But more important than the pain is my love for you.
I love you.
I will carry you.
You will overcome this.
Just know
I WILL NEVER LEAVE YOU!
Just know
I WILL NEVER LEAVE YOU!

Surrender You to Death

I remembered your touch when I cried;
The most pleasurable sensation around.
It was like a kiss from Heaven,
Calming my heart from the storm.
But now my eyes are never dry,
And my breath has left my chest,
For your touch, I'll never feel again
I have surrendered you to death.

It Was Only Lip Service

I believed you.
You offered something better.
You made promises.
You told me what I wanted to hear.
It was only lip service.
My wall was up.
You brought it down.
I let in you.
I had hope.
It was only lip service.
I knew better.
The wall was up for a reason.
Damn me for trusting.
Damn you for lying.
It was only lip service.
You left quicker than you came.
I honestly didn't expect it.
I believed you.
Why? I knew better.
It was only lip service.
I have begun to reconstruct my wall.
I will use stronger bricks this time.
My mortar will be like cement.
The wall will be unbreachable because,
It was only lip service.
Damn you for lying.
Damn me for trusting.
I didn't need this journey.
Why did you lie?

Why did you leave?
It was only lip service.

Summer Turned to Fall

Twas the first day of my summer,
As into adulthood, I rolled.
The magic of possibility around me
Shown bright, promising, and bold.
Of the shining, alluring, splendid,
Of what my future could be,
Shaking the shackles of youth,
For once in my life, truly free.
But what does a youth
Know of liberation?
What do they know of great joy?
How do they appreciate their new station?
And with folly and short understanding,
My summer quickly became fall.
Bound to a new contract.
Foolishly, I traded it all.

Half a Tear

Half a heart, half a tear,
Half a year to get over,
All in the name of love;
Broken, nothing left over.
"Build the wall, close the heart!
Don't let anyone in!"
Into the valley of sorrow,
because I let you in.

Relationship Blooming

The joys of relationship blooming—
Men and women being stupid—but alive
Making life worth living
The once dying now thrive
The heart once again giving...
-unaware of the heartbreak dooming.
The thrill of new relationship beholding—
Passion overtaking—flowing
Inside and out
Seeds of hope sowing
Love and trust does sprout...
-yet the breakdown already unfolding.
The change comes in, unbeknown-
Pain swaps out happiness-cheated
Hurt, fear, and sadness
The good feelings depleted
The happy mind overtaken by madness...
The lover left alone.

Give Them Forever

When you love someone and they become your obsession,
And everything you do is to make a good impression.
Just get on you knee and ask the greatest question.
And give them your life forever.
Give, give, give them forever.
Give, give, give them forever.
Give, give, give them forever.
Because you believe in love.

She Rules for Her Sake

She demands tribute from those in her control.
Unwilling to consider their needs.
Pushing them into her black hole.
Entangling them in her manipulative weeds.
She says she does it for them,
While hiding her true intention.
Really, she has a self-gratification stem.
Her subjects in need of intervention.
Though she will always claim she is saintly.
With toxins, her ways are dripping.
As she is self-focused, injuring greatly.
As their confidence, she is stripping.
Dictators like her cause deep heartache.
As she rules for her sake.

Where Is...

Where is the friend loyal and true
Who said they'd never leave?
Where is the teacher dedicated to teach
When none of the content makes sense?
Where is the preacher full of grace
Who turns their back to mistakes?
Where is the government to rule by democracy
When they cheat and abuse power?
Where is the parent dedicated to home
When the house always feels empty?
Where is humanity
When the desolate lives in the gutter?
Into a place that evokes tears,
Into a place where hearts do fail,
Into a place of loneliness and lies,
It's time to step up and create change.

A Mistake that You Made

You will see couples and remember me,
And recall the love I gave.
Optimism and hope will play on their faces,
As you recount all the kindness I bestowed on you.
You long for the kisses they share,
As your body feels my last touch.
When the couple disappears into the setting sun,
You will drop to your knees,
And cry that you let me go.

As Our Relationship Turns to Dust

When were last together
You saw me in your light,
A promised friendship forever,
A unity ever bright.
Since then, I've born my soul,
To the real me trapped inside.
Acceptance is my ultimate goal,
No longer wanting to hide.
Though few have stayed with me,
Most friends have closed the door.
All because I let myself be.
I've lost my friends from before.
Flooding me with sorrow,
More than the rest,
You closed down our tomorrow,
Your disapproval you've expressed.
Unchanging is my value.
My personality the same.
I can't handle your displeasure,
As you now treat me with shame.
I suppose I'll go on living,
As our friendship does combust.
I'll work on my forgiving,
As our relationship turns to dust.

Losing their Greatest Friend

One cannot undo
What one has did
How can one compensate
Losing their greatest friend

O Heart

The courageous heart,
Yet a heart of untruth.
I cannot trust you, Heart.
O Heart, you led me chasing.
Chasing the wrong way.
You misjudged.
You misguided.
Now I don't know what to do.
O Heart, why do I believe you?
Why do I allow you to take me here?
I must be wary of you, Heart.
I must not answer your call.
Why do you set me to fail?
O Heart, you lift me on a high.
O Heart, you chop the legs beneath my being.
You are unworthy of my attention.
I must cage you.
I must wall you off.
O Heart, I'll turn you to stone.

Casually Tossed

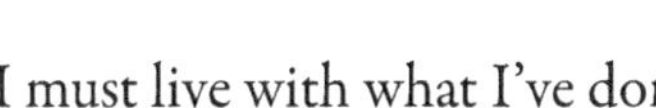

I must live with what I've done.
A moment lost in the fun.
It only takes a little bit.
To throw your life in a pit.
I want to reclaim what I've lost.
The best of my life -casually tossed.
I should have been more ethically sound.
I should have kept my desires bound.
But I coveted what wasn't mine.
I crossed over the dividing line.
Now I must live with my sin.
I lost it all when I gave in.

Spiritual

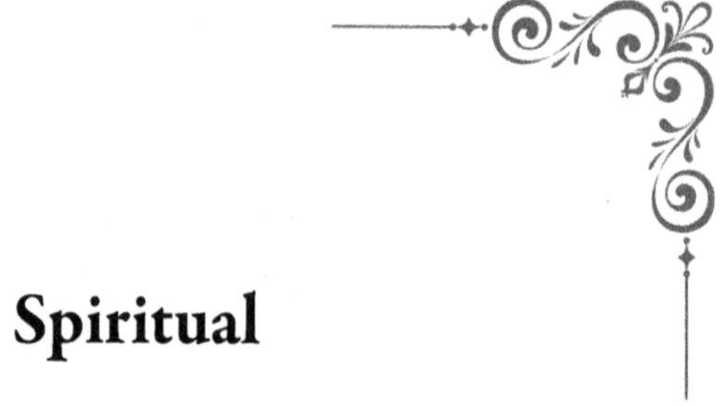

On Her Knees

Breaking her promise
Looking for something elsewhere
Never settled
Chasing lies
She finally finds peace on her knees.

Kneel, Bow, Kneel

The tension hangs in the air,
As discord flares the land.
The time is now to turn to God,
As Christian values are banned.
Kneel, bow, kneel; take the time to pray.
Kneel, bow, reflect; remember God all day.

We fail; we wail.
At times, we lose our way.
There's much to confuse,
As evil tries to sway.
Kneel, bow, kneel; take the time to pray.
Kneel, bow, reflect; remember God all day.

We must unite,
As Christians take a stand.
Our values to cling tight,
Supporting hand in hand.
Kneel, bow, kneel; take the time to pray.
Kneel, bow, reflect; remember God all day.

Holidays

It's hard to honor the holy days
When they become the holidays.
The people run around in a maze,
Subcoming to the commercial ways.
How to worship the Lord above,
How to give out the proper love,
When people push and shove
And think of God, only kind-of.
The holidays have turned cold,
With consumerism to uphold,
And propaganda bold,
Just so products and goods get sold.
It's hard to honor the holy days
When they become the holidays.
The people run around in a maze,
Subcoming to the commercial ways.

Trust in God

Peace of mind, peace of soul.
Peace flowing around me.
All from the Lord above.
Your kindness astounds me.
"Let Him in, trust in God!
Hold to the rod."
Into my will, I mold you.
You, the mighty God.

God's Gift from Above

God's precious child
Warmed hearts when she smiled.
But when the rainbow colors she donned,
All the adulations to her were gone.
Her value remains inside her,
Thou other's opinions deter.
Regardless of how she defines love.
She'll always be God's gift from above.

She Judges

While the commandments she does follow,
While idle sin, she does not wallow,
While taking meals to the needy,
Even giving without being greedy.
She holds herself on a pedestal,
With her religious efforts, she does befool.
She appears perfect without smudges,
Yet everyone else she harshly judges.

Amendment

Out of the hold of the mind's deception,
Stronger than the will of the heart,
Spanning from thought's conception,
The warped mental shreds hope apart.
Assessing the soul's simple pleasures,
Harder to find each day,
Blocking life's countermeasures,
The desperate has gone astray.
Pushing out the dark matter,
Clearer the mind ascends,
Ignoring the negative chatter,
The lost spirit comes to amends.

Nature

The Loss of the Netherlands' Coastlines

The construction company controls the coastline,
While their top concern is their bottom line.
The Dutch preserve their coastal aggregate mine,
While destroying Norfolk and Suffolk shoreline.
They are annihilating the fish's spawning lifeline.
While the dredging is causing marshes to decline
And eroding beaches' skyline.
Another sad story as ethics decline,
Devastating the Netherlands coast sea-line.
All for the mighty dollar sign.

Machu Picchu

Machu Picchu, you call me.
Early Inca's royal estate.
Where did they go? What was their fate?
Did they all die, or did some flee?
They left artifacts and debris.
Their mountain offers an astounding view,
Of the majestic land of Peru.
This is where the Inca reigned.
With cut-out terraces, life sustained.
The mighty Incas of Peru.

Black Widow

Such magnificent beauty.
Exquisite.
None other can compare to her.
She holds my attention.
I should leave.
Staying this close is deadly.
But I can not pull away.
Her lure has locked me in, enamoring me.
I move closer.
I want to touch her.
But I can't.
That would be death.
I want to capture her and display her.
I shouldn't.
Logic tells me to kill her.
She isn't safe to keep around.
How can I destroy such a fascinating creature?
I always thought I would be frightened if I encountered one.
But her grace thrills me.
I want to study her.
She glides toward me, those long, elegant legs.
I want to touch her.
My children giggle in the background.
She is not safe to have around.
What if she bites them?
I hate this choice.
Her life, or theirs?
I should let her live.
She most likely will never meet them.

But what if she does?
She comes even closer to me.
I bring my head nearer to her.
Wow, she entrances me.
How can I kill her?
How can I let her live?

By the Light of the Moon

Hike- Not prepared
Hike- Some scared
Hike- No light
Hike- No others in sight
Hike- Byson next to the trail
Hike- Please don't impale
Hike- Seems extra long
Hike- Must stay strong
Hike-By the light of the moon
Hike- Will be done soon

Southern Utah

Landscape of red rock and hoodoos.
Slot canyons and adventures.
A warm, dry wind blows.
Sun rays shrivel the vegetation.
Adventurers set off.
Water bags strapped to backs.
Feet marinating in sweaty shoes.
Foreheads glistening.
Ropes set.
Repels and climbs.
Moving along dry riverbeds.
Wading through stagnate puddles.
A scrape here, a cut there.
Wedging through tight places.
Skipping in vast canyons.
Southern Utah-
Earthly heaven.

Only Winter and Nothing More

While in my room, I rested, frozen in bed, my mind infested,
I wanted to get up and move. Is that too much to ask for?
As I imagined, nearly dreaming, in came the light, brightly streaming.
In the light, I remembered opening the door, a better life beyond the
door-
"It's only winter," I muttered, "so why do it I abhor?
Only winter and nothing more."

Then my energy spiked; It's the coziness I liked.
I pulled myself out of bed, bringing my quilt to the chair.
As I moved, my spirits lightened, feeling fresh, my joy heightened.
At the hearth, I started building, building up a fire-
"Tis time to snuggle," I uttered as my happiness moved higher.
"Only winter and nothing more."

While in the chair, my puppy joined me, its warm body snuggling in
tight.
Beyond the window, the snow drifted, drifted behind the door.
As I watched, the fire blazed; I relaxed in my place.
"I do love winter," the words repeated, repeated in my head-
Comfy and cozy with my companion, the words rang in my head-
"Cuddling is what winter is for."

Winter, What Would You be

Winter, what would you be
Without skiing and sledding,
Through the freshly fallen powder,
Sparkling, swirling around?
Winter, what would you be
Without hot chocolate and
Cozy fires?
Winter, what would you be
Without ice hikes and
Snowshoeing?
Winter, what would you be
Without Christmas and
All the brilliant lights and
Holiday cheer?
Winter, what would you be
Without snowball fights
And snowman creations?
Winter, what would you be
Without ice-skating on a frozen pond?
Winter, what would you be
Without fishing on a solid lake?
Winter, what would you be?
-I dar'st want to know.

Winter, a Season that Sparkles

When the grace of the universe gathers,
A collection of positive energy flows.
-Winter, a season that sparkles.
Once here, the world slows.
When the lights in the heaven
Paint the sky to the north,
A color show so splendid,
Illumination and color burst forth.
And in the dens of the mighty bear,
Sleepiness does subdue.
Their bellies filled for the winter,
The mighty beast does snooze.
As the cold covers the living,
When the plants bury deep in the land,
Whiteness glitters with brilliance.
-Winter's glory does expand.

Florida Can't be Beat

As the sun blesses vegetation,
As the manatees move in migration,
As Florida sustains life,
The greatest place in the nation.
People flock to the blessed place.
Filled with diverse cultures and race.
Sweeping the country, Florida can't be beat.
Blessing the land with oceans and heat.

Only a Rainstorm and Nothing More

While on the beach, the tourist played, or in the surf, they swim and
wade.
Leaving all their troubles home, they release their stress at our shore.
Without warning, almost sneaky, in comes the storm, dark and
streaky.
In the rain, tourists crawl behind their car door, hiding behind the
door-
"It's only a Florida storm," I mutter as the heaven pour-
"Only a rainstorm and nothing more."
In my yard, the rain does stream, creating the Florida dream.
I watch my kids grab the shampoo, showering under the storm's roar.
Acting abash, tourists drive by, while in the puddle, my kids splash.
In their joy, my children playing, imagining in the rain-
"'Tis only children," I mutter as the tourist complain -
"Only a rainstorm and nothing more."
At the parks, the rain does soak, drenching the common folk.
The people buy ponchos while hiding behind a door.
As I watch, residents keep playing while the rains continue spraying.
In my joy, I love the storm, as the word repeats in my head-
"It's only a Florida storm," I mutter at the tourist's dread-
"Only a rainstorm and nothing more."

When Nature Called to Me

Because I could not stop for Nature,
Her storm blew down a tree;
Somehow, I was too busy
So Nature came to me.
When did it happen?
Outdoors, I used to be,
But the corporate boardroom
Is now all that I see.
Staying indoors always,
now only the walls I see.
I had closed my heart to Nature.
My spirit, no longer free.
So Nature sent a summer storm,
to shake the forces be.
Her majestic power,
Nature calling to me.
The lightning flashed and rumbled,
the waves rocked in the sea.
The powerful summer storm,
brought Nature back to me.
I missed my time outdoors,
my only true therapy.
It was time to return to Nature,
When Nature called to me.

Celestial Arizona Night

Stars shine brighter above Havasupai.
Washed out is the heavens in the cities,
Skies devoid of life beyond.
Yet the Arizona desert doth capture the eye.
Behold the stillness of the Arizona night,
As toads croak their melody,
And creatures scuttle in the sand.
Above, the stars twinkle in brilliant light.
No place on earth can compare,
As shooting stars streak the sky,
And darkness moves in shadowy crags.
-To the splendor of the celestial Arizona night air.

Ode to Winter

Twilight of life coming to a slower pace.
Light from the sun appears less often.
Lifeforms fattening and hunkering in place.
White flushes out color, making things soften.
Where is the energy that fuels the land?
Trees and plants are dormant; will they return?
What of the children who played outside?
The vast emptiness leaves the heart to yearn.
Only in dreams, summer vacations planned.
Hoping for hikes and warm days on the sand.
But today is winter, where everything died.

Grow, Thrive, Grow

Creation falls across the land
As the summer crop thrives.
The gardener waits in anticipation
For onions, tomatoes, and chives.
Grow, thrive, grow; harvest time at hand.
Grow, thrive, pick; the harvest preserved and canned.

So crisp, how sweet; A garden treat.
The hard work begins to pay.
Enjoy it fresh, such a delight.
Save some for another day.
Grow, thrive, grow; harvest time at hand.
Grow, thrive, pick; the harvest preserved and canned.

Oh, what a delight, the baskets full,
With fruits and vegetables splendid.
Soon fall will come, and sadly
The growing season ended.
Grow, thrive, grow; harvest time at hand.
Grow, thrive, pick; the harvest preserved and canned.

Open Stretch of Prairie Ground

As tumbleweeds move across the plain,
As the parched land cries for rain,
As the antelope gather to feed,
This is where the spirit is freed.
The open stretch of prairie ground,
Offers respite from the city sound.
It's time to answer its persistent call.
Surrendering yourself to its all.

Springtime Came Pushing

The raindrops battered the window with a tap-tap-tap if you please.
Dust and pollen stirred by the moving of the breeze.
The flowers freshened the air, with their colors on display.
And springtime came pushing-
Pushing- pushing-
Springtime came pushing,
Winter out of the way.
Baby animals made their appearance with a bray-cry-whimpering
sound.
The plants sprouted from seed out of the unthawing ground.
Children left their houses to go outside and play.
And springtime came pushing-
Pushing- pushing-
Springtime came pushing,
Winter out of the way.

Women's Issues

Her Light Does Dim

She can't figure this world out.
What the hell is life about?
When she gives, her intentions are questioned.
Some turn it away, which feels like rejection.
Others are critical of all that she does.
They seem to hate her just because.
Every choice she makes is criticized.
Her very being unrighteously analyzed.
If she gives, then she gives too much.
If she loves, then it's unwanted touch.
She serves with all her heart.
But her intent they rip apart.
Her goal is to make others better.
But her personality they try to fetter.
Slowly, her light does dim.
Once hopeful, now her outlook is grim.

Her Value Halted

She's middle-aged
That's how she presents
She's middle-aged
Her back, slightly bent
She still feels young
Though her knee now buckles
She still feels young
Even with arthritic knuckles
She avoids the mirror
Her face has changed
She avoids the mirror
Feeling slightly deranged
Why does youth pass
Her status, no longer valued or exalted
Why does youth pass
Her value halted

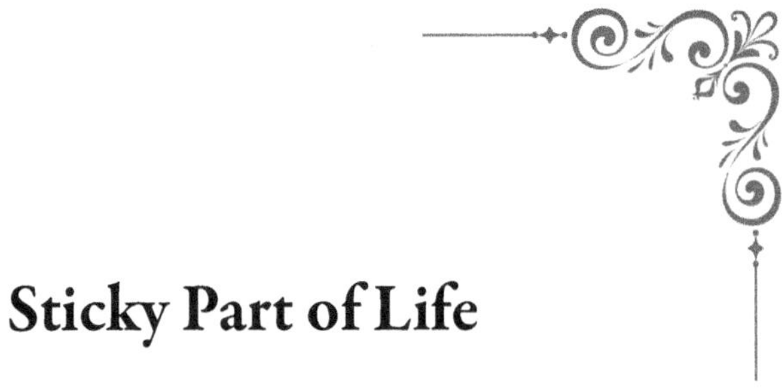

Sticky Part of Life

Clean Energy Scheming

While on my couch, I rested, laid out, my mind infested.
I wanted to change the environment. The thought of clean energy did
implore.
As I imagined, nearly dreaming, in came the ad, manipulation
scheming.
Clean energy, the ad peddled, teaching fossil fuel to deplore.
"Only you can make the change," they muttered, "against fossil fuel,
let's go to war.
A Tesla car and nothing more."

Then my anger spiked, the pundits' dishonesty I disliked.
As Musk pushed his electric Tesla, Space X burned fossil fuel galore.
Musk's carbon footprint imploding, with each launch, 29,600 gallons
of rocket fuel unloading.
Yet, in the ad, clean energy was their promised lure, teaching fossil fuel
to abhor.
"Tis only hypocrites," I muttered, "lying from their core-
Only a push for wealth and nothing more."

Taken

Once a field of green, lush and wonderful;
Now, a stretch of asphalt.
Once trees climbed to the lowest cloud;
Now, a chain-link fence.
Once a stream branched in several spots;
Now a cement ditch.
Once sky blue and clear;
Now air brown as dirt.
Once we played outside;
Now, everyone confined in the house.
Once we reverenced Mother Nature;
Now, electronics is our God.

-In the Name of a Pandemic

They stole from us our freedom
-In the name of a pandemic
They lock us in our homes
-In the name of a pandemic
They limit the number of people in stores
-In the name of a pandemic
They obliterated millions of people's livelihoods
-In the name of a pandemic
Gyms closed
-In the name of a pandemic
Trails fenced
-In the name of a pandemic
Playgrounds barricaded
-In the name of a pandemic
Borders shut
-In the name of a pandemic
Unemployment increased
-In the name of a pandemic
Liberties altered, changed, robbed
-In the name of a pandemic
They ration what we can buy
-In the name of a pandemic
They restrain our medical options
-In the name of a pandemic
They cripple our economy
-In the name of a pandemic
Families burdened
-In the name of a pandemic
Debt incurred

-In the name of a pandemic
They sealed schools
-In the name of a pandemic
They destroyed lives
-In the name of a pandemic
They shattered dreams
-In the name of a pandemic
Weddings called-off
-In the name of a pandemic
Funerals denied
-In the name of a pandemic
Churches shut down
-In the name of a pandemic
Missions aborted
-In the name of a pandemic
Graduation ceremonies halted
-In the name of a pandemic
Travel restricted
-In the name of a pandemic
Media frenzy
-In the name of a pandemic
False information
-In the name of a pandemic
Social norms dismantled
-In the name of a pandemic
Restrictive laws
-In the name of a pandemic
Relationships stalled
-In the name of a pandemic
Nations weakened
-In the name of a pandemic
Establishments barred

-In the name of a pandemic
Gatherings ended
-In the name of a pandemic
Progress deadlocked
-In the name of a pandemic
Sports canceled
-In the name of a pandemic
Teams dissolved
-In the name of a pandemic
Panic instilled
-In the name of a pandemic
Government control increased
-In the name of a pandemic
First Amendment rights suspended
-In the name of a pandemic

...

...and we let them
-In the name of a pandemic

Human Race on Edge

2021, the year of panic.
Who would have predicted such mayhem?
The human race on edge.

A pandemic no one understands.
Policies made from fear versus facts.
2021, the year of the panic.

Stay-home orders; people are restless.
Race wars; hate and anger spreading.
Who would have predicted such mayhem?

Social norms changing.
Riots and mass confusion.
The human race on edge

Tolerance

I demand tolerance!
(you must think like me)
I demand justice!
(my needs trump yours)
I demand respect!
(you're doing it wrong)
I demand equality!
(you must put me first)
I demand peace!
(I'm uneasy with you here)
I demand the right to protest!
(your voice we must silence)
I demand a platform
(you are reprehensible)

Why

When will this end?
-the panic
Where did science go?
-manipulate
Who is in control?
-politically driven
Why can't it just play out?
-must drag it on slowly
When does mental health count?
-many dying inside
Where is the control?
-in the fear they manipulate
Who does this hurt?
-most everyone
Why do we follow?
-choices taken
When does the lost business count?
-collateral damage
Where is the truth?
-ever changing
Who benefits?
-State funding
Why?
-because they lie

Then You are Better than Most

If you can avoid the political theater,
Or ignore entertainers' lewdness while performing at theater,
And disregard un-graces while at the movie theater,
Then you are better than most.
If you can stop religious mumble spilling out your throat,
Or refrain from judging others as a religious cutthroat,
Or in a battle of words, you don't go for the throat,
Then you are better than most.
If you can stop putting others in their place,
Or refrain from entering a shady place,
Or hold onto your values even if you lose your social place,
Then you are better than most.

Yet, We Must Still Resist

Tonight, in Myanmar, my wife works alone
As the children cry for rice.
She will rise to care for my mom at least three times.
On this humid night, sweat will drip into her eyes.
My mom will fight her daughter-in-law.
It should be me who cares for my mom.
Tonight, my wife will watch the door,
Her hands picking at her scabs, anxious for my return.
She will have to bravely kill any cobras or vipers,
Although they terrify her.
The noises of the night will keep her awake,
Since I am not there to protect her.
Tonight, I sit surrounded by others,
In a dilapidated jail cell.
The bugs feast on us, and we cannot stop them.
We marinate in our waste as we stack upon the other.
We tried to resist the coup d'état
staged by Min Aung Hlaing.
Tonight, I am a prisoner who fought against the foe.
My comrades and I revolted,
Little to no avail.
Just hours ago, two brothers died,
And their families still don't know.
We had to do something, but our defeat made it in vain.
Tonight, I wonder if I will ever see my family again.
How many widows will be left with a family they can't support?
How much infliction can we Burmese take?
And now we are prisoners, stripped of all we are.
Demoralized by the foe,

Yet, we must still resist.

Strong Citizen Take Stand

Do you conform in the pressure of the crowd?
Knowledge and truth discarded by the side;
Rage, rage against the head bowed.
How do the educated follow like sheep,
Relinquishing freedom without thought?
Do not sell your soul for that which is cheap.
Good men, the last wave, must stand and unite,
Educating others, the key.
Rage, rage against the distinguishing of light.
The authoritarian will never stop trying to take,
Their promises never fruition.
Do not succumb; do not break.
Grave citizens, tired citizens, unite and energize.
If you do not fight, then who will?
Rage, rage against the lies.
Strong citizen, take a stand, or freedom dies.
If you do not fight, then who will?
Rage, rage against the lies.

Awake My Citizen

Awake my citizen, and you shall see,
All the forces that don't want us free,
Of propaganda misguided,
For the purpose of making us divided.
Come together, my citizen, and open your eyes,
Entanglement and falsehoods filled with lies.
Of agendas to control,
To confuse us is the goal.
Awake my citizen and see the truth.
Defend the rights of the aged and youth.
Hold to the truth. Take a stand.
Fight for your nation and your land.

2022 Haikus

MONKEY HOLD
Harassed on the street
Gangs of macaques take over
Rouge- monkey city

LIFE FOREVER ALTERED
Expressions silenced
Populations locked indoors
Life changed by COVID

GLOBAL WARMING
World overheating
Glaciers melting and shifting
Global warming scars

Democracy Divided
Discord felt at home
Neighbors against each other
Political split

History

Eastern Gate Route

Expanded by Han dynasty
To connect the Asian Society
Trade products along the route
Traveled often by a scout
Aided development of civilizations
A passageway between the nations
Political relations expanded
Commodities bartered and branded
Exportation and ideas exchanged
Religious mission's passage arranged
Empires built and destroyed
New ideas along it employed
Plagues moved through like fire
Multiple continents able to inspire
One long path connected the East
Aided commerce and ideas to increase
The gateway to move goods about

Esteemed Silk Trade Route

My Lai

Let my heart hold a moment of silence for you.
-A peaceful village filled with families who cared for and loved each
other.
What was your crime?
-Accused of being Viet Cong sympathizers.
My Lai.
Not a draft-age male found among you.
-Calley, your executioner.
Calley had a decent youth.
What happened?
How did he become so evil?
Women were raped.
Babies slaughtered.
BABIES!!
Were those babies VC sympathizers?
Weren't we there to protect them?
My Lai.
How to excuse the idea of collateral damage?
You are not collateral damage.
You are humans.
You have wants.
Wishes
Dreams.
How did we become so evil?
How could we close our eyes and destroy you?
No heart.
No empathy.
Pure slaughter.
Was Calley innocent?

-Just following Medina?
Can we close our consciousness off in the name of orders?
Thompson didn't.
Thompson showed bravery.
But it was mostly too late for you.
My Lai.
I can't understand how "decent American men" could
Switch to rapists and murderers.
What is the color of our hearts?
Do we change who we are in the name of orders?
Where's our accountability?
History is full of this brutality.
The present-day still has this.
But for us Americans, we feel so pompous and Godly.
Aren't we above this?
My Lai.
I can never bring you back.
My heart hangs low for you.
My Lai.

Yersinia Pestis -What's Happening?

Lymph nodes tight and swollen.
-what's happening?
Head pounding out of control.
-this is frightening.
Muscles contracting as the vomit spues.
-what's happening?
Appendages turning black.
-this is frightening.
Pain unbearable.
-what's happening?
Did a flea really bite me?
I don't recall this happening.
Yes, there are mice in my house.
But I did not touch them.
Body shaking, can't make it stop.
-what's happening?
Skin burning, fever so high.
-this is frightening.
Blood comes out when I cough.
-what's happening?
Ugly buboes on my skin.
-this is frightening.
So sick, will I die?
-what's happening?

Revolutionizing the Spread of Information

O printing press, O Printing press
A form of knowledge dissemination
O printing press, O Printing press
The spreading of information
Not only did you revolutionize
Your power opened the political eye
O printing press, O Printing press
A form of knowledge dissemination

Benjamin Banneker

What's so important about quiet Benjamin Banneker?
The wake he created during his Time,
A self-taught man of color, mathematician, and Astronomer.
-Rising above racism and ageism; upward he did Climb.

He was recognized and loved by the Abolitionists,
Who promoted the work of his Almanac.
Their love for freedom made them true Partitionists,
And hallowed his work and his star gazing Knack.

Benjamin so humble, a mind sharp and Bright,
Even corresponded with Thomas Jefferson.
His almanac he gave, and about his brethren, he did Write,
Advocating for others and freedom for Everyone.

His intellect showed there is value in all Skin,
When we start seeing that, then everyone will Win.

Fritz Haber

O Fritz Haber! O Fritz Haber! rise up and see the starving masses;
For you, a challenge to bring nitrogen to the land —for you, the Nobel
Peace Prize in hand;
For you, they call, your genius mind, your fertilizer, oh so grand;
Here Fritz Haber!! Dear Savior!
Your invention created in your head;
Turned biochemical warfare,
Millions fallen cold and dead.
Fritz Haber! Human life has no measure;
Fritz Haber has no morale; appeasing the Reich has its pleasure;
The treaties in place, you ignore and break;
Your biochemical warfare leaves death in its wake;
Fritz Haber, your fertilizer delivers life, yet you give other gases.
But many, with mournful dread,
your legacy,
saves and yet leaves others dead.

Yersinia Pestis

Today, we call it the Black Death.
Medieval times called it Blue Sickness.
An epidemic spread by living breath,
But mostly flea vectors flow of viscous,
Causing fevers, chills, and extreme weakness.

If diarrhea was all you got
Consider yourself one of the few blessed.
For other's appendages blackened and rot,
While the growth of buboes progressed.
Yersinia Pestis, it fury behest.

Pneumonically, the droplets carried,
And through fluids, the Bacillus is spread.
-Three forms, unique yet varied.
A bacteria, bringing nations great dread.
And leaving two-thirds of the population dead.

Through centuries, they could only fear the plague,
As it brought countries to their knees.
Their knowledge to fight it was too vague.
A pandemic spread by a simple sneeze,
Or when one got bit by an infected flea.

Today, antibiotics can curve this beast.
And we see fewer transmissions.
The death toll has decreased.
And even though Yersinia Pestis is not in full remission.
Thank goodness for medicine and physicians.

Mores Code

Mores Code
Dots and dashes
Mores Code
Early radio communication
Mores Code
The opening of the information age
Mores Code
Proficient way to communicate
Mores Code
Used in the air and the sea
Mores Code
Lives are saved
Mores Code

Panama Canal

As he crossed the Isthmus, the idea did form.
-A way to avoid the coastal storm.
How would this land Balboa transform?
A passageway could save months at sea.
-His proposal as the canal's conferee.
An easier passage he could foresee.
But nothing happened until hundreds of years later.
When along came a French innovator.
With the loss of life, Lesseps was a poor estimator.
USA picked up where Europe and France failed.
They architected the idea to scale.
They thought their plans they had detailed.
They could not predict the high death toll,
As they tried to build a massive hole.
They'd have to get this under control.

In all, over twenty-two thousand people died.
For this great oceanic stride,
To effectively carry ships to the other side.
Despite the death, disease, and war,
Carter, then Wilson, the idea to restore.
January 1914, the lock opened its door.
Alexandre La Valley, the first in the canal to cross,
By using the canal, it saves thousands of miles lost,
Keeping sea-hands and passengers from exhaust.
The Panama Canal is a miraculous feat,
Saving time and money for the oceanic fleet,
Making the loss of months at sea obsolete.

Let's remember the lives sacrificed for this gift,
That makes traveling around the states swift.
When we think of it, let our gratitude lift.

Window C

Leave all your effects at window C.
Leave all your affects for them to see.
They'll rummage, they'll plunder, they'll take, they'll keep.
They'll rummage, they'll plunder, try not to weep.
They already took your life and home.
They already took all that you own.
These are the last of your meager belongings.
These are the last of your dreams and longings.
Place on the counter your final possessions.
Place on the counter your relinquished professions.
Pajamas will cover your naked frame.
Pajamas can't cover your burning shame.

Cortez

Oh Spanish Conquistador.
Off in search of your own.
You were a land invader.
Lime lighting as a mere trader.
Gaining the native's trust.
Really, you were a nadir.
In God's name, a crusader,
Pulling down their religion.
Doing it in the name of their sin.
You were a land invader.
You let death be your campaign.
While their lands you did gain.
You, Cuba, tried to arraign.
They were boiling mad; it's known
For your treacherous feign.
But you were loyal to Spain.
You formed Vera Cruz, your Flagstone.
And from the Aztec, you did gain.
Their freedom you held in a chain.
The things you did were disgust.
For you, their land was a must.
Their life you did retain.
It didn't take much for you to win.
Raising yourself high, their kingpin.
How'd you do it, how'd you win?
How did their nation you did gain?
Their fortresses you broke in,
With deception and your grin.
Your status, a parader.

The number of your men was thin.
Not having much to begin.
Your guns took you to the throne.
And your horses, against stone.
With your deception built in.
The things you did were unjust.
Annihilating them to dust.
Oh Cortez, such a disgust.
For the gold and the win.
With your plans, you did thrust.
All their art you did combust.
And all the gold you did attain.
Their homes you burned to a crust.
And temples you did readjust.
Oh, Spanish Conquistador
You became a slave trader.
Leaving the Aztecs to blood and bone.
Annihilation, full-blown.
You took over, creating your zone.
Raping the woman with Spanish lust.
The Aztec ways no longer known.
Your hearts as cold as stone.
Your life a testament of sin.
Did you ever atone
For the deeds you have sown?
Against a nation and its pain,
Your wave of horrific bloody reign
And taking over the throne?
Oh, Spanish Conquistador
The new land invader.
You are a degrader.
The Aztecs are mostly unknown.

All their ways, you did combust.
Burying everything within
As their nation was slain.

Colonial Rum

As they take the native's land,
As their tribes they try to disband,
As they hold no value for their life,
A method better than the knife.
They dupe the natives for a swig of rum.
The strong drink makes the Iroquois numb.
Sweeping in they take it all.
Watching the beguiled natives fall.

William Williams Keen

William, you are a hero unsung,
Yet kids chase after men with balls.
But, your name should be on the lips of the young.
Your image plastered on their walls.
William, serving in your 80th year,
A time when most men need to rest.
But, serving our finest with your medical gear,
Saving the lives of our military's best.
William, why should we all know your name,
From your hundreds of publications?
But, those are just a piece of your acclaim,
Pioneering skills that shaped nations.
William, you were the first in the surgical field.
-Like removing a tumor from a brain.
But, your success continued to wield,
The first to cranial fluid drain.
William, how did you feel,
When you massaged the open heart?
But you continued to find ways to heal.
Your methods a medical art.
William, what would the medical field have done,
Without your first colostomy performed?
But, your achievements had only begun.
The medical field transformed.
William, the first to suture a damaged nerve,
And the jaw of President Cleveland you saved.
But, people keep your name on reserve.
As your place in history has been shaved.
William, you've done way more than addressed.

Your achievements shaped our lives.
But, our medical advancements you blessed.
Let's honor your life-changing strives.

Chance Favors the Prepared Mind

Because he had prepared to learn,
A desire for discovery inside did burn.
Pasteur, a renowned French Biologist,
A chemist turned pathologist.
Chance Favors the Prepared Mind
Diseases prevented because of Louis Pasteur.
His progress fights against the bacteria war.
While rabies once had no cure,
It's neural assault, the bitten forced to endure.
Chance Favors the Prepared Mind
Pasteur opened his intellectual thought.
He learned, experimented, and he taught.
With his mind always learning and astute,
He directed the Pasteur Institute.
Chance Favors the Prepared Mind
His Germ theory made great waves,
And think of all the lives it saves.
The simple process of sterilization,
Teaching about germs and causation.
Chance Favors the Prepared Mind
Think about how wine did sour.
Microbes, multiplying by the hour.
All you have to do is add some heat,
Which makes bacteria almost obsolete.
Chance Favors the Prepared Mind
We learn to stay sharp by Pasteur's example.
Keep on educating your hippocampal.
Always be prepared to learn something new.
Then inspiration will come to you.

Then inspiration will come to you.

Spartacus

Built for combat excellence at Lentulus Batliatus' Gladiator school,
Held captive against his will,
Trained in methods for excellent showmanship in the ring,
was the slave known as Spartacus.
To subjugate those who were not of pure blood was the Roman way.
Even Partar-familia of Roman lines could go as far as selling or
enslaving his child if choosing.
Romans, egotistic, high-minded, and idolatrous, took pride in
destroying other's lives.
Spartacus was one such slave.
But Spartacus had other volitions for his life.
A natural leader, he convinced at least seventy fellow slaves at the
school to revolt.
Grabbing whatever they could in the school, turning the contraband
into weapons,
Pugnaciously fighting their way free from oppression.
Victory! Free, and yet not, they escaped to Mount Vesuvius.
Swelling his ranks, Spartacus liberated more slaves,
Welcoming men of the land, his army grew to 70,000.
Senates of Rome underplayed the power of this man.
Attacking, Romans dispatched legions of soldiers,
Only to be defeated again and again.
They couldn't have this: a slave against the Senate.
Romans fought, Spartacians battled.
Egos swelled as Romans prevailed.
Senerchia, the land of the annihilation of free-will, free-spirits.
Freemen.

To be free is the noblest of dreams.
Spartacus died defending his earthly rights,
And the inherent prerogative of other slaves.
No man should enslave another.

Propaganda

Oh, Propaganda, congratulations!
I send to you dearest adulations.
For through you, the most innocent has been dubbed.
You were used by the great Roman leaders.
Deception laid out by Julius Caesar,
Polluting the minds with his agenda.
The Spanish Armada knew your mendacious tricks.
-The great vice of Queen Elizabeth's politics.
They used false, slanderous pamphlets and letters.
A College of Propaganda was set up.
The heathen ways they planned to clean up.
Directed by Pope Urban the VIII.
You influenced the French Revolution.
Voltaire and Rousseau played a contribution,
As they opposed France's Bourbon Rule.
Gandhi arrested for the things he taught,
Like civil disobedience and boycotts.
His use of you got him jailed and shot.
Hitler's propaganda beguiled a nation,
As the Germans blindly followed his dictation.
Because of you, millions of lives were lost.
Religions thrive because of the use of you.
You tell them what's evil and what's true.
Blindly, they construct their lives from your word.
Today, most opinions you've shaped.
Your influence everywhere has never escaped.
Cleverly drafted, you rule the world.

Lobotomy

Turn you into

Who we want

You to be

Not right

In the head

As all can see

A few

Small holes lets

The demon free

Conforming you

To be

Like me

Of course

It's not done

Too hastily

A way to
Release your
Anxiety

It's okay
If it leaves
You sleepy

It's a fail
Safe
Surgery

We must
Perform with
Urgency

You must be

Changed

We all agree

Oh

Sadistic

LOBOTOMY

Don't miss out!

Visit the website below and you can sign up to receive emails whenever Stephanie Daich publishes a new book. There's no charge and no obligation.

https://books2read.com/r/B-A-IQHV-TATNC

BOOKS 2 READ

Connecting independent readers to independent writers.

Also by Stephanie Daich

Alora Funk
Alora Funk - The Deliverance

Standalone
Out of Breath
Life Chapbook
Phoenix on Fire
World on Fire
Asp

Watch for more at https://stephdaich3.wixsite.com/
phoenix-z-publishing.

About the Author

Stephanie Daich sees life as a gift and opportunity for experience, discovery, and growth. She dabbles in a little bit of everything, including writing. She interacts with the world through the written word and exploration, continuously learning as much as she can cram into a twenty-four-hour period."The most significant commodity is time, and we should never waste it."

Read more at https://stephdaich3.wixsite.com/phoenix-z-publishing.

www.ingramcontent.com/pod-product-compliance
Lightning Source LLC
Chambersburg PA
CBHW060924140726
47996CB00001B/364